John Foley.

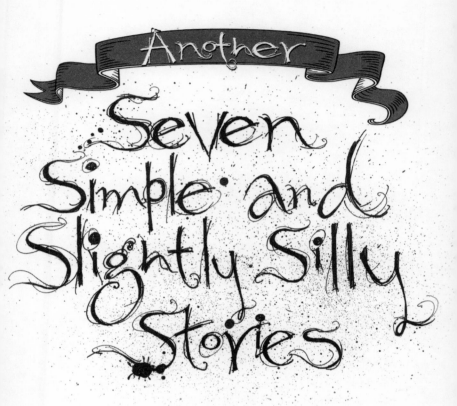

Another Seven Simple and Slightly Silly Stories

John Foley

Drawings by Grant Cathro

QuizzicalWorks

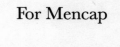
For Mencap

Contents

The Snooty Puddle

One day, not so long ago, there was a puddle in the middle of the road. Rain had been falling for several hours and the road – more a lane really – was in a bad state with scattered potholes and cracks from one end almost to the other. To the left of the puddle in question – let's call it George for the sake of argument – and to the right of it there were other puddles. Most of them were larger and one or two were much larger, but to our puddle slap bang in the middle they were of no consequence, because although George was quite small it was deeper. It also had in it flecks of gold.

To begin with, George didn't know anything about this, and probably would never have known anything about this had it not been for the rain stopping, the sun coming out, and two old women. The women had completed their shopping and, heavy laden with their bags, were returning home. Halfway down the road they paused to look at the potholes now filled with rain.

'It's disgraceful, that's what it is!' complained the older of the two. 'All these holes and cracks, and does the council take a blind bit of notice? Does it fooey! There'll be a nasty accident along here one of these days.'

'Wouldn't surprise me,' agreed the younger. 'When I think of poor old Mr Taylor on his bicycle and how he suffered with his broken–' Suddenly she stopped as she noticed the sun glinting on George's surface. 'Oooh, look at this one! It's all sparkly.'

The older woman, who had a vivid imagination, drew nearer. 'Oh, yes!' she said. 'Like it's full of flecks of gold.'

'Flecks of gold! Oh, you have such a way with words. "Flecks of gold",' she repeated admiringly.

'Wouldn't it be lovely if it was gold?' said the older. 'I could do with some of that right now, I can tell you. Put it in a bottle, sell it to someone and I'd be so rich.'

'*We'd* be so rich, I hope you mean. I saw it first, remember?'

'And I'll be happy to share it with you!' laughed her companion. And then with a sigh and one last wishful glance at George she moved away, and the younger one followed. But the matter didn't end there, for as they continued down the road, they discussed – as one inevitably does on such occasions – how rich they would both be if only life was fairer, and all the things they'd spend the money on, until they were so out of earshot that a fascinated George could hear no more.

Now, however strange this might seem, it so happened that George had heard about gold, about how it was a noble metal that was precious and highly prized in almost every part of the world. And because of the golden flecks the two women had talked about George started to think that he (it seems churlish to call him 'it' from hereon) must be very special, even noble like the gold itself. And the more George thought in this lofty way the more he wanted to let everyone know, and so, rather snootily, he began to voice his thoughts. Initially, the other puddles took no notice. After all, why should they? But no one likes a braggart, and eventually one of the larger puddles shouted: 'Give it a rest, will you!'

'Don't you speak to me like that!' George shouted back. 'I'm special, I am! I've gold in me!'

'Gold!' snorted a puddle a few yards to the right. 'Whatever gives you that idea?'

'You heard what those women said.'

'Don't tell me you believe their twaddle?'

'And why not?' said snooty George. 'I bet they've seen more of the world than you have.'

'Hark at that one!' sneered a puddle to the left. 'You've no more gold in you than that lamppost!'

'How would you know?'

'Because I've seen gold, and I've seen rust and I know one from the other.'

'Rust?' said George.

'Common or garden rust, that's what you've got,' sneered the puddle more forcefully.

'How dare you!' cried George.

'Contaminated!' shouted a puddle from further along. 'That's what you are!'

This silly banter might have continued for some time, but just at that moment a car turned the corner and hurtled down the road, sending water from the larger puddles spraying to either side and trickling down the gutters.

'Ha! Serves you right!' said the snooty puddle, safe in the middle. But his triumph was short-lived, for as the afternoon wore on and the sun grew hotter three dreadful things happened in the road – and to George in particular.

Whenever and wherever puddles and young children come together there's likely to be only one outcome, and this occasion with two children on their way home from school was no exception.

'Oh no, don't!' cried George, as the two screamed and stomped and splashed through each and every puddle with glee and gusto, and especially through the deepest one, which was of course our snooty puddle. 'Please, please, you don't know what you're doing! Stop that!'

But the children didn't understand puddle, and even if they had been able to understand it's doubtful whether they'd have taken much notice, delighted as they were with their game. Eventually, however, they tired of the splashing and stomping and went on their way. For a short while afterwards there was a lull, and George, exhausted and somewhat drained, pondered on the unfairness of life.

Occasionally, birds would come to drink from the puddles and even bathe in them, and in their own odd way the puddles were happy to be so used. But no birds visited snooty George. No, not one. The birds were wary of him and his rather strange water.

At first George was more than happy with this. 'See!' he cried, as one after another the birds approached and then backed away and hopped elsewhere. 'They know class when they see it!' But after a while he began to feel slighted. 'What about me?' he moaned. And then a bit later: 'It's not right. It's so not right!'

'You wanted to be left alone!' cried the puddle to George's left.

'Well said!' cried the puddle to his right. 'You wanted to be left alone!'

'Yes, but not ignored like this!'

'You can't have it both ways!' said the puddle to his right.

'Yes, I can. I can!' George insisted. 'I'm special.'

'Specially stupid, if you ask me,' laughed the puddle to his left.

'Barmy!' said another puddle.

'Nuts!' said a fourth puddle. And from further down the road came the judgment from a fifth: 'Crackers!'

'Oh, you!' cried George, who was beginning to feel really hurt by such appalling and unwarranted treatment. 'You... you... you're just jealous!'

Surprisingly, this accusation shut them all up, and for a moment or two they began to wonder if there was something in what George said. Perhaps they *were* jealous. Perhaps George *was* special and he really did have gold in him. But then, almost as soon as they thought this thought they realized that such a thing was impossible, and almost with one voice they burst out again with a fresh attack on George and his claims.

By this time poor George was quite demoralized, and if he could have slunk away he would have done. But he couldn't; he was stuck where he was. Feeling small and grossly unappreciated, he decided his best course of action was to keep silent. Let them call him silly names and belittle his specialness, he would not say another word. And he would have stuck to this resolution had it not been for the dog staring down at him.

A mangy, ugly brute of a creature: the sort that obviously couldn't make up its mind as to what breed it would like to be. It stared for a while, and George stared back angrily, glaring and scowling with all his might, as if daring the cur to come any closer. For a brief moment his glaring and scowling took the dog by surprise. It jumped back, woofed a bit, cocked its head, and even had it in mind to lollop off to a friendlier puddle.

'I should think so,' muttered the snooty puddle, believing his reaction had done the trick. 'Good riddance, you mangy brute!' But George spoke too soon, for just when he thought he had won the battle, the dog lowered its head and began to drink greedily, and oh so noisily, slapping the surface of George's by now not so precious water with its big ugly pink tongue. Oh, the indignity of it!

But worse was to come. Attracted by the woofing

a second dog rounded the corner. Sensing that there was clearly some fun to be had leaping in and out, and possibly to gain a cool soaking at the same time, the second dog joined the first, and a new game of splashing began up and down the road and in and out of every puddle, much to the delight of them all. All that is apart from George, who once again seemed to be the favourite target.

'Stop that, go away!' shrieked George, with a power that surprised even him. But his protestations were to no avail.

Eventually, as so often happens when the fun goes too far, the game between the two dogs became a tussle that became a fight, and if one of them hadn't decided that enough was enough and run off to be chased by the other, who knows where it might have ended? As it is, George was even more exhausted, and even more drained.

'Ohhh,' he moaned to himself. 'How could this happen to me? To me, who is so special. Is there no justice in this cruel world?'

Fortunately, he had the sense on this occasion to keep his thoughts to himself. But even if he had been heard the other puddles would have taken no notice, for they themselves now had their own worries. During the course of the afternoon the hot sun beating down on them had taken its toll. Slowly but surely and bit by tiny bit, the shallower puddles began to shrink as the water in them dried.

'Well, time to go!' the puddle to George's right said philosophically.

'Go? Go where?' said George.

'Dunno, mate. Where we all go in the end, I suppose.'

'But where's that?'

'Never been there, have I? So how would I know?'

And the next moment the puddle was gone.

'Perhaps we're off to a better place,' another puddle suggested. And before George could ask where this better place might be that puddle was gone, too.

The final straw came sometime later that afternoon in the form of a rather large, bad-tempered crow. Having sampled some of the few remaining puddles and found them not to its liking, it now approached the snooty puddle and lowered its head.

'Oh, no you don't!' shouted George, and once more he glared and scowled with all his watery might, even more than he'd done with the dog. The crow took one look, then backed away crossly, and for a moment George thought he'd succeeded. But then the crow approached again and, with an irritable cawing noise, turned its back on George and… yes, you've guessed it. 'Oh!' wailed George, as the crow did this most despicable thing. 'That is disgusting! Where are your manners?' All of which of course was completely wasted on the bird.

The matter should have ended there but George, now outraged, made such a fuss and became so rude and so vociferous, hurling every insult he knew (which sadly for him was not many), that the first crow was soon joined by another, and then another and another, till George found himself surrounded by brother and sister crows and their relations all venting their spleen on him. Who knows how long this desecration would have continued had it not been for a lorry bearing down on them? With a final vent the crows scattered and poor George was at last left alone to bemoan his fate. 'Oh, the shame of it! To sully my golden waters in that foul, abominable way.'

'Golden waters?' called a puddle weakly from nearby. 'Are you still on with that–?'

But then it too was gone, and the road was silent.

'Hello? Anyone there?' called George, and answer came there none. 'But you can't all leave me!'

Night fell. A warm night it was, and now, where not so long ago the bright sun had sparkled on the puddles, there was a bright moon. Despite its coolness George could feel himself shrinking, becoming shallower and smaller by the hour. 'No, no!' he muttered to himself. 'Surely I'm too special, too precious just to disappear like the others. And if I do, what will happen to my golden flecks?'

Just after midnight a dark cloud appeared in the sky. George's hopes soared. Saved, he thought. But the cloud passed on. 'No, no, wait!' he cried. A second dark cloud appeared, but it too passed on. George began to despair. A third cloud appeared. Darker than the first, darker even than the second, it covered the moon. 'At last! Rain, oh please, rain and save me!' George begged. As if the cloud had heard, a few drops fell. 'Yes, yes!' cried George. 'More, more!' And as his confidence grew and he thought he felt the water rise, he cried out: 'Haha! Told you I was special!' But the cloud evidently had better plans and moved away.

The night wore on, and George grew weaker and sadder and lonelier. There were no children to splash about, no dogs to drink from his surface, not even a disgusting crow to rail against.

As the rays of the early morning sun shone on the puddle and dried the last damp patches, George remembered the cruel words of the other puddles: 'You're just like the rest of us but with a bit of rust.' And in his last moments he realised how wrong he was to have presumed himself special and to have wasted his–

Finally, where the snooty puddle had once been there remained only some light-coloured flecks. Here and there they were certainly slightly reddish, but elsewhere unmistakably golden.

The Wisdom of Teaching Reindeer to Read

The trouble began with the alphabet. Correct me if I'm wrong, but it's reasonable to suppose, isn't it, that a human – child or adult, male or female – learning his or her alphabet can be only a good thing, and often even a benefit to mankind as a whole? But to teach the alphabet to reindeer? There, surely, you're asking for trouble. And that's just what transpired with Donner and Blitzen.

Before you get too judgmental, see it from Sid's point of view: Sid being Sidney Christmas, better known to some as Father Christmas, to many others as Santa Claus and perhaps to other others as something else. However he's known, Sid's an enlightened fellow, an optimist who naturally sees the good in everyone and hopes always for the best. As far as he's concerned, anything that improves the lot of man or beast – be it spiritually, culturally or whatever – must be good. But there, unfortunately, he was wrong.

The idea of teaching reading to his beloved reindeer came to him one afternoon in late summer, when the hours of sun were still long and the evenings and nights almost so short that they were over before they'd even started. At such times of inactivity Sid was especially fond of reading. There was nothing he liked better than to curl up on a sofa indoors or in a comfy armchair outdoors and immerse himself in whatever book he could lay hands on. Fiction or non-fiction? It was all the same to him. If he was in the mood for a good read, the sort of book mattered not.

On this particular occasion he was halfway through a rather silly comic novel, the sort that made him laugh out loud and often. Donner, Sid's favourite reindeer, was puzzled. What, he wondered, could there possibly be between the pages of that book that could cause such laughter? And having wondered that question he ambled over to ask it.

'What exactly is so funny?' he said.

'Ah, well, you see...' said Sid, and for the next hour or so he explained the plot and the how and the why of his merriment. Although Donner didn't really understand Sid's explanation (reindeer are not noted for their sense of humour), and in fact he secretly thought it all rather silly, now that he'd broached the subject he was curious to learn more about the black dots, lines and squiggles on the page that his mentor found so delightfully interesting.

'Letters,' Sid explained.

'Ah!' said Blitzen, Sid's second favourite reindeer, who had wandered over to see what Donner was up to. 'Like what we deliver sometimes with the presents?'

'No, those are very different,' said Sid. 'These ones are all letters of the alphabet. There are 26 of them—'

'Twenty-six...?' queried Donner, for whom anything over eleven was a number too much.

'Most of the time, yes. In some languages there are more and in other languages fewer,' Sid continued. 'But however many there are, when you put them together they make words. Like this...' And taking his walking stick he traced the letters D-O-N-N-E-R in the snow. 'There... that's you.'

Donner stared hard at the tracing, then walked round to look at it from the other side. Finally, he said rather crossly: 'Huh, it doesn't look like me.'

'No, no, no,' said Sid. 'That's your name. See the different shapes?' And he spelled them out again.

This time Donner almost did see. And he was impressed. 'Oh my... that is something,' he murmured at last. 'Yes, indeed!'

'I should say so,' said Sid.

'And that is really me, my name?'

'No one else's,' said Sid.

'Oh my!' Donner murmured again, now even more impressed and more than a little proud.

Having finished his explanation Sid was about to turn back to his book when Blitzen nudged him hard. 'Do me, do me!' he said.

And so Sid, never one to refuse his reindeer, traced Blitzen's name. To begin with, Blitzen was confused about the patterns in the snow which, apart from the 'E' and the 'N', were not at all like Donner's, and it took some time for Sid to convince him that the various shapes represented sounds, and that the sounds in the two names were different because the names were different. All this, of course, is elementary, but to someone like Blitzen it was quite a leap to take in in one go. When at last he thought he understood he laughed out loud, and kept on laughing for several minutes.

Meanwhile, curious as to what the laughter was about, the other reindeer – Dasher, Dancer, Prancer, Vixen, Cupid, Comet, young Rudolph and even Smudge, the most junior of them all – left their stalls or wherever else they were at the time and wandered over. And, not unnaturally, once they discovered what was going on, they too wanted their names spelled out (all, that is, except for Cupid who was only interested in food and soon wandered away again). Encouraged by such interest, Sid put down his book again, and for the next few hours patiently traced the names in the snow with his stick, all the while explaining to the assembled company the different sounds of the vowels and consonants.

To say that they were enthralled would be bending the truth. In fact, apart from Donner (who considered the patterns in the snow for his name the most interesting of them all) and Blitzen and possibly young Smudge, they were not much bothered either way, and eventually they too drifted off to find something more worthy of their time.

Now you may or may not be aware of this, but not only were Donner and Blitzen the best of friends, they were also the best of rivals. If one of them did something, then the other had to do it too, and to do whatever it was just as well, if not better. And so it happened with reading. To tell the truth, Blitzen couldn't be less interested in the dots, lines and squiggles, but he certainly wasn't going to admit that to Donner. If Donner was going to learn to read, then he too must learn.

And so it began.

When Sid's wife Peggy, or Mrs C as she was known to the reindeer, heard about what was going on she was none too pleased. It is accepted in many parts of the world that behind every great man there's a strong woman to guide him, to keep him steadfastly on whatever track he should be (or on whatever track she thinks he should be), and Mrs C was no exception. A kindly woman, she had a heart of gold. But it was gold tempered with steel. She it was who ruled the roost as far as the reindeer, the elves who worked throughout the year preparing the presents for the great day, and all the other helpers who made Christmas possible were concerned, and woe betide anyone, her Sid included, who dared to contradict or annoy her. So when Sid mentioned the reading lesson later that evening she made no secret of her alarm.

'You did what?' she demanded.

'It was just a few letters here and there,' he protested. 'Nothing too advanced.'

'You're asking for trouble, Sidney Christmas!' she

told him with a wagging finger. 'Teaching them to read. Whatever next?'

'Come, come, my sweet. A little learning never did anyone any harm.'

'A little learning in the wrong hands can be a dangerous thing. Filling their heads with fancy ideas. Ideas above their station! Mark my words, in no time at all they'll be demanding shorter hours and more food!'

'Oh, surely not. They know their place.'

'They won't know their place if you confuse them with this nonsense!'

'I don't agree,' said Sid. He puffed his pipe for a moment, then added, 'and anyway, who are we to begrudge them a little more brain power? Donner's coming on a treat with his alphabet; he can even say it backwards.'

'Fat lot of good that'll do him in a snowstorm,' snorted Mrs Christmas.

'Talking of fat,' said Sid, 'Cupid has been on at me again about too little to eat.'

'What did I tell you?' said Mrs C triumphantly. 'It's started already!'

'Aha!' her husband replied, equally triumphantly. 'Cupid is the only one who has spurned it all from the word go. Why,' he chuckled, 'greedy old Cupid wouldn't know his name in the snow from a hole in the ground! Wouldn't know his ABC if it jumped up and bit him in the bum!'

'Sidney! Don't be vulgar!' said his wife.

'What? Oh, yes. Sorry about that, my dear. Getting carried away.'

'Well don't!'

Suitably chastened, Sid went off to inspect one of his many workshops.

Of course matters might have rested there and the whole incident been soon forgotten if Sid had taken heed of Mrs C's warning. But he didn't. Once started he became quite excited by the prospect of having reading companions, someone to share his books with (Mrs C was never a likely candidate). Over the next few days he became so occupied with teaching first the alphabet and then ever so slowly some of the rudimentary whys and wherefores of the written language that he quite forgot the silly comic novel that had started it all.

But while Donner revelled in each new day's discovery Blitzen found it more than a bit too much, and gradually he began to tire of learning. 'This is all very well,' he thought to himself one evening a week or so later, 'but what's the point of it?' Having asked that question he came to the conclusion that there wasn't any point, and for the first time in his rivalry with Donner he gave up. 'If that's how he wants to spend his time,' he muttered, 'then let him. I don't care.'

And yet... and yet something about what Blitzen had learnt so far caught in his mind and niggled and tickled there like an annoying itch. It was there that night when he went to sleep; it was still there the next morning.

'What is it?' he cried out so loudly that Cupid in the next stall raised his head from his third breakfast.

'Eh?' he asked.

'Oh, you wouldn't understand,' Blitzen said gloomily.

'Probably not,' Cupid agreed, and went back to his munching.

Later that day, Blitzen determined to shake off the niggling suspicion he knew was there but couldn't quite grasp by going for a long, long walk through the snow. But it didn't work; still the feeling persisted. The further he walked, the more irritated he became for ever having started on such a pointless venture as reading and writing with its petty details like the order of letters and... Suddenly he stopped dead in his tracks, and his mouth dropped open as he realised what had been bothering him. 'Aha!' he cried at last, 'that's it!' And without another thought he rushed back to where Sid and Donner were struggling over the different spellings of the words 'rain' and 'rein' as in 'reindeer'.

'Yes, they do have the same sound,' Sid agreed.

'So why not spell them the same?' asked Donner, rather crossly.

'The alphabet!' panted Blitzen, as he swerved to a stop. 'Show me again!'

While Donner was none too pleased by this

interruption, for Sid it was a welcome break. Patient to the last, he began for the nth time to repeat the order of the letters, both vocally and with his stick: 'A, B, C, D—'

'Stop!' cried Blitzen when Sid got to D. Sid stopped, and Blitzen thought for a moment. Finally, he said, 'Why?'

'Why what?' asked Sid.

'Why A, B, C, and so on in that order?'

'Hmmm,' said Sid, 'I never thought of that.'

'Because it's such a dumb question,' said Donner, even more crossly.

'No, no, not at all,' said Sid. 'Blitzen has a point there.'

'So, it's a good question?' asked Blitzen, feeling rather proud.

'It's actually a very good question.'

'Aha, how do you like that then?' said Blitzen, pleased to get one up on Donner. 'It's actually a very good question.'

'Fine,' said Donner. 'So why then?'

'Why what?' said Sid.

'Why is it A, B, C... and all the rest of it in such an order?'

Sid was flummoxed. 'You've got to have some order, haven't you? After all, think of the chaos without it.' He turned to the well-loved dictionary he always carried now. 'Look,' he said leafing through the pages, 'see how easy it is to look up a word such as… such as…'

'Chimneypot?' Blitzen suggested.

'Excellent choice!' said Sid. 'Now we know that 'chimneypot' begins with the letter C and that C comes after B, so we can go straight to that section of the book without floundering all over the place. Similarly, we know that the next letter H comes after G, so–'

'Yes, but why that particular order?' asked Blitzen. 'Why not… F, W, Z, O, and so on? Or P, T, M… etc?'

'Because that's the way it is,' said Sid, somewhat ashamed at such a poor response. 'Tell you what,' he added, 'let me do some homework, and if I find a better answer I'll come back to you. How's that?'

'All right,' said Blitzen gloomily.

'Fine!' said Donner. 'And now that's settled can we get back to my lesson?'

'All right,' said Blitzen gloomily again, and he wandered away to think some more.

You've probably realized that although Blitzen was a bit of a thinker, he was not the quickest of thinkers. It could take time for information not only to filter through his brain but for him to make sense of that information. He knew he'd stumbled onto something, but precisely what that something was continued to elude him, and when he went to bed that night he was still none the wiser.

A good night's sleep can work wonders with niggling questions, but in Blitzen's case it didn't. He was none the wiser the next morning, or the morning after that. As the weeks passed the niggling also passed. And then just when he'd almost completely forgotten about whatever it was that had bothered him he awoke one morning to find the answer staring him in the face. 'Of course, yes, that's it!' he cried out so loud that Cupid awaiting his breakfast in the end stall raised his head to ask: 'What's it this time?'

'Oh, you wouldn't understand.'

'Probably not,' muttered Cupid, and went back to waiting.

By now the long lazy days of summer were over and it was time to start preparing for the busy winter months and the great night – the one night in the year when Sid and his stalwart team would be stretched to the very limit.

It was the custom at this time of year to begin practice runs with the sleigh, to help build stamina for the journeys ahead. This had happened year after year after year for as long as any of them could remember, and this morning was – or should have been – no different.

'Morning all!' cried Sid cheerily, as he entered the stable. 'Rise and shine, rise and shine!'

'Morning,' they all mumbled, some more sleepily than others.

'Right, let's make sure we're all here, shall we?' This procedure was quite unnecessary as there was certainly nowhere else for them to be. However, as a way of starting the day, they liked it and he liked it. He began calling out the names in pairs as he always did: 'Donner and Blitzen?'

'Present and correct and raring to go!' Donner said as he always did. Normally Blitzen would have answered with equal enthusiasm, but this time there was only silence.

Sid paused, unsure if he'd heard correctly. He repeated the question. Again Donner responded loudly and confidently, but still from Blitzen came no answer. Sid was immediately worried.

'Blitzen, my dear chap! What is it? Is something the matter? Are you ill?'

'Nothing's the matter and I'm very well, thank you. In fact, I couldn't be better.'

'But why didn't you answer when I called your name?'

'For the simple reason that I can no longer accept that order.'

'Order? What order?'

'According to you B comes before D. Is that not so?'

'In terms of alphabetical order, yes,' Sid agreed.

'So it stands to reason you should say Blitzen first and Donner second.'

'You what?' cried Donner. 'You're not serious?'

'I certainly am,' said Blitzen.

Here there was a muttering and mumbling from the other reindeer, none of whom had any idea what Blitzen was talking about.

'It has further come to my attention,' Blitzen continued, 'and here I must give thanks for your valuable teaching, that it is not merely in alphabetical terms that I have for countless years been wrongly coupled but also in meteorological terms.'

'What are you on about?' snorted Donner.

'Yes, what are you—?' said Sid, before correcting himself. 'I mean to say, I don't understand.'

'Blitzen means lightning, right?'

'That's true.'

'So you named me after lightning?'

'Yes.'

'And he's Donner, after thunder?'

'That is correct. Why do you ask?'

'Because it's always "Donner and Blitzen this", "Donner and Blitzen that".'

'It does sound rather good, doesn't it?'

'It does not!' exclaimed Blitzen. 'It makes no sense. How can thunder come before lightning? It doesn't work that way. It can't work that way. You have lightning then you have thunder.'

'Ah, I hadn't thought of it like that. Interesting,' said Sid. Hoping that that was the end of the matter, he moved on down the line. 'Prancer, good morning!'

'Not so fast!' said Blitzen. 'I'm not finished yet.'

'Can we get a move on?' said Cupid. 'I want my breakfast!' And with further mumbling and shuffling some of the others agreed.

'Allow me to elucidate,' said Blitzen.

'Ah, no... can I stop you there? Just for a moment?' said Sid.

No doubt you've gathered by now that Sid, Mr C, was a fairly mild man, a man who shied clear of conflict whenever he could. But he was by no means stupid, and he recognized that this was a new Blitzen, a Blitzen he had never seen or heard before. As such, he knew also that he was out of his depth. 'Everyone, please, we'll continue our roll call later,' he said, 'but for now do enjoy your breakfasts. Blitzen, perhaps you and I had better discuss this with Mrs C.'

'As you wish,' said Blitzen. He started out of his stall and began walking out of the stable in the direction of the house.

'Just a minute!' cried Donner. 'This involves me as well, doesn't it?'

'Yes, I suppose it does,' agreed Sid. 'Perhaps you'd better come along, too.'

As soon as Mrs C saw her husband and the two rather determined reindeer she knew there was trouble.

'All right, all right,' she said. 'What is it?'

But before Sid could explain, Blitzen did so for him,

telling her that he refused to be coupled with Donner in the old way, and that from now on if their names came together he would only respond if his came first, as was truly correct.

To say Mrs C was flabbergasted would be a mild way of putting it. For a moment she was speechless; but only briefly. The next moment she exploded.

'I don't believe it! There, Sidney Christmas! Didn't I warn you?'

'Please don't blame him,' said Blitzen. 'I've been thinking about this for some time, and I've come to the conclusion that it's only right and proper that unless this matter of… what did you call it, Mr C, when you put one before the other?'

'Precedence,' mumbled Sid.

'That's it, yes! Unless this matter of precedence is settled I have no alternative but to withdraw my services as one of your team.'

'Well, I'm certainly not going second!' said Donner. 'It's always been "Donner and Blitzen", and as far as I'm concerned "Donner and Blitzen" it shall remain.'

Mrs C glared at Mr C, as if to say 'I told you so', but before he could mumble a word in his defence she turned her glare on Blitzen. 'And this is your ultimatum, is it?' she asked.

Now it was Blitzen's turn to be speechless. He had learned many new words in the last few months but 'ultimatum' was not among them. Sensing this, Mrs C went on the attack:

'Ah, so you don't know everything, do you?'

'I think she means–' began Mr C, in an effort to smooth the way a little.

'She means you're talking mutiny!' said Mrs C. 'And I don't care if you don't know that word either. But I tell you this: if you don't give up this reading lark and all this precedence nonsense, you're off the team and I shall have to find replacements! You, too, Donner!'

Blitzen had not expected this or anything like it (nor for that matter had Donner), but having come this far he felt he could not back down. 'I–' he began, but Mrs C was too quick for him.

'Not another word! I'll give you till teatime to come to your senses. Off you go now, and have a serious think. But remember: I can't afford to keep passengers. Either you work or it's off to the butcher's for you both.'

'The butcher's?' said Sid. 'Peggy, my dear! You're joking, of course?'

'You know me, Sidney. I never joke,' she replied, and sadly this much was true. 'Well, away with you!'

Somewhat weak at the knees from Mrs C's attack Donner and Blitzen went their separate ways to have a serious think. Without the two of them to lead the sleigh, the practice run was cancelled, and they and all the other reindeer spent the hours at a very loose end.

Teatime came, and so did Mrs C. 'Well?' she demanded, striding into the stable. 'What's it to be?

Will you give up this nonsense and get back to work?'

'I will if he will,' said Blitzen.

'Deal,' said Donner grudgingly. 'But I still go first.'

'Nooo!' cried Blitzen. 'I will not have it!'

'Er, perhaps...' said Sid hurriedly, before Mrs C had a chance to explode. 'Perhaps I could suggest a compromise?'

'Eh?' said Blitzen.

'What if you alternate? Each Christmas one of you goes first, and next Christmas the one who was first goes second, and the one who was second goes first. That's fair enough, don't you think?'

'So who's first now?' asked Blitzen.

'Me!' said Donner.

'I think not,' said Sid firmly. 'This year it must be Blitzen's turn.'

'And that's your compromise, is it?' asked Donner.

'It is indeed,' said Mrs C, speaking for her husband. 'And a very good one. Take it or leave it. But remember what happens if you leave it. I hear smoked reindeer is very popular these days.'

There was an audible shudder around the stable, and not least from Blitzen and Donner. They looked at each other, then at Sid and then at Mrs C, who had the sort of determined look on her face that did not bode well for the wrong decision.

'I'll take it,' said Blitzen at last.

'Donner?' demanded Mrs C. And if it's possible for a reindeer to look sheepish, he did. 'Me, too,' he said finally.

So the matter was settled. The two rebellious reindeer went back to work, and in no time at all they were the best of pals again. And much to the satisfaction of Mrs C, somewhat to the sadness of Mr C, but greatly to the relief and delight of the rest of the team, from that day to this Donner and Blitzen – or rather, Blitzen and Donner – have not looked twice at a book.

Young Smudge, on the other hand... but that's quite another story.

The Squirlybird

Who on this extraordinary planet can fail to notice and even to marvel at the wonders of nature? On land, in the waters, in the air, live creatures of the oddest shapes, and of sizes from microscopic to gigantic, with some surviving in the harshest and most improbable conditions. Strange, weird, ugly, beautiful – nature has the lot.

One of the oddest and most striking of them all was the squirlybird. Certainly in the air he had no equal: he was swifter than a falcon and could fly farther than an albatross. Where other birds' wings beat up and down (and his beat faster than a hummingbird's), his rotated; round and round they swivelled in such a blur that they could hardly be seen. Most of the time this action propelled him forwards, but he could just as easily fly backwards or sideways. Sometimes, to feel the sun on his breast, he would even fly upside down. His powers of flight were beyond compare: hovering, soaring, darting, diving; he did them all and with such ease. He could swim, too, and not only on the water but under it. For defence, he could puff himself up to more than three times his size, and in that fearsome state could growl like a dog or snort like a wild boar – if such were ever needed.

And, if all that were not enough, he was as handsome a creation as you can imagine and his plumage was more gorgeous and rainbow-coloured than a bird of paradise.

Among his other talents, the squirlybird could talk. Nothing special in that, of course. All birds talk in one way or another, and how they talk! He was different. No idle chatter for him. When he had something to say (which was most of the time) he said it with style. No matter the subject – fact or fiction – he knew what to say and how best to say it. His telling of news and stories was a delight. Wherever he travelled he would listen to whatever was happening, and if he deemed it of note would retell it (colourfully embellished) days, weeks, months later to a fresh audience. As for his composing verses – comical and tragical – he was a master. Yes, when the squirlybird appeared, birds (and other animals, too, for he would happily talk to anyone) would gather from miles away to be enthralled by his tales, his honeyed words, his mellifluous tones. As one rather jealous gull remarked, the squirlybird could charm the wings off a dodo (though, considering the source, this remark was probably not a compliment).

In short, he was everything a bird could be, and had everything a bird could have – except for one thing, as you'll shortly discover.

Of course, as is so often the case, admiration for this wonderful creature was not universal, and it was only a matter of time before envy reared its head. It happened like this. He had just flown in to a favourite resting place and had as usual been welcomed with

delight. Word spread among the locals that he had an exciting new tale, and in no time an expectant audience assembled. He was about to begin when two magpies appeared, perched on a nearby branch and started clacking in the very ugly way that magpies do. The audience tried to shush them, but the magpies were out for mischief.

'Rubbish!' cried the one.

'Yeah, rubbish!' cried the other, the more aggressive of the two. 'Why waste your time listening to his nonsense?'

'Because he's the greatest!' piped a young fan.

'The greatest? You're joking!' sneered the first magpie.

'If he's so bloomin' marvellous,' sneered the second, 'how come he can't sing?'

'Eh?' said several of the audience.

'Can't sing?' said several others, believing such a charge was impossible.

'Not a note!' clacked the first magpie.

''Course he can sing!' cried the young fan, to whom the squirlybird was so wonderful that nothing was beyond his talents.

'Bet you he can't!' said the first magpie.

'Bet you he can!' the fan insisted. 'Come on, Squirly. You show 'em!'

'Yes, give us a quick song to shut 'em up,' cried another of his admirers, 'and then we can hear your story.'

And here… yes, you've probably guessed it, was the problem. If there was one thing this remarkable bird could not do, it was sing. He had always known that he couldn't, and on the surface it had never bothered him. After all, when you already have so much going for you why demand more? Deep down, however, the failure worried him. Up till now no one knew about it, but he had always feared that one day his luck would run out. Suddenly this was the day.

Spurred on by the magpies, his audience was becoming restless.

'Story, story, story!' came from one section.

'Song, song, song!' came from another, and all too soon those calling for the former were drowned out by those demanding the latter. The squirlybird realized he must do something. He also realized that there were only four options: he could refuse to sing and insist on telling his story; he could collapse in a dead faint; he could flee; or he could sing. Quickly he evaluated the four: the first was pointless; the second would only delay the dreadful moment; the third would certainly lay him open to accusations of 'coward', which would merely reinforce the suspicion that he couldn't sing; while the fourth would prove beyond all doubt that he couldn't. Faced with this decision, he opted for the last. After all, how bad could it be? So, he cleared his throat and began to sing.

The effect was stunning. Never had such an awful sound been heard or even imagined. It was worse than the harshest honk or squawk. There was a gasp of astonishment. With an embarrassed laugh and a muttering about Saharan sand in his windpipe the squirlybird apologized, cleared his throat once more and tried again. But if anything, this second attempt was worse than the first, and now the astonishment changed to howls of dismay. Even the young fan who knew the squirlybird to be so wonderful that nothing was beyond his talents was appalled, and if he could have wept he would have done.

'Told you he's rubbish!' clacked the magpies gleefully, and having completed their mischief they flew off.

The squirlybird flew off, too. With his pride wounded and humiliation ringing in his ears, he flew and flew and flew till hundreds of miles separated him from the scene of his failure. And then quite suddenly he stopped in mid-air. 'This is ridiculous!' he thought. 'I'm extraordinary, I'm remarkable, I can do anything! And if there's something I can't do does it really matter? Huh, it's only singing! Who needs it? I don't!' And so saying, he resolved that from then on it would not be an issue. He would continue in his own highly successful way, and if anyone ever commented about his inability, he would answer: 'So what? I don't sing, and there's an end to it! Now do you want to hear my story or not?'

Sometimes, however, such resolutions are easier made than kept. The seed had been sown, and as seeds planted in fertile soil invariably grow strong, so this one grew. He began to fret. By day he thought of little else but his failure; at night his dreams were plagued with the magpies' clacking.

No doubt you've heard the expression 'a little bird told me'. And that's how it was: a little bird told a big bird who told another bird who told another bird and so on and on, until there was scarcely a bird in the world who did not know what had happened.

The crunch came just a short while later, and again before an audience. He had just embarked on a story about an ancient land that disappears under the sea, when a mockingbird flapped down. As the name implies, mockingbirds (who can mimic almost any sound) are not the kindest of souls, which the squirlybird now found to his cost.

'Haha!' laughed the mockingbird. 'If it isn't mister-can't-sing-a-note! Not so wonderful now, are you?' And he began imitating the squirlybird's hideous singing. He couldn't do it as badly (even the most accomplished of mockingbirds couldn't equal that), but it was bad enough. The audience fled. And with the dreadful sound harsh in his ears the squirlybird fled, too.

For the poor squirlybird the cruel taunt was the last straw. Out went his resolve not to care, and in its place came a craving so fierce that he would gladly have exchanged his looks, his wit, even his powers of flight for the gift of singing. By nightfall his anger had cooled a little and he started to think more clearly. 'It can't be that difficult,' he reasoned. 'After all, if dull, common birds can learn to sing, so can I. Just a case of finding the right teacher.' Cheered by this thought he shook off his humiliation and very early next morning went in search of one.

By chance, the first bird he came across was a blackbird who, in the spirit of the dawn chorus, was in the middle of an especially sweet song. The squirlybird listened transfixed, entranced by the beautiful melody pouring forth, seemingly so effortlessly.

'How lovely! How delightful!' he enthused once the song was finished.

'Ah, a true music lover!' said the blackbird. 'Care for another?'

'You mean there's more?'

'Oodles more!' the blackbird replied. And happy to oblige, he launched into another song, which to the squirlybird's hungry ears seemed even more exquisite. Never had he heard such music; never had he imagined that any creature could create such beautiful sounds. Finally, the blackbird stopped and, after enthusing with the highest praise, the squirlybird asked, 'How do you do it?'

'Singing? It's easy. I just open my throat and out it comes.'

'And that's it?'

'As far as I know. I've always done it like that.'

'Can you teach me to do it?'

'Teach you? I wouldn't know where to start.'

He tried a robin next, then a nightingale, then a skylark. Seeking help, he flew from one corner of the Earth to another, from west to east, from north to south. But always it was the same story: none of them knew how to teach him. In his travels he even quizzed birds who couldn't sing (of which there were so many more than he expected). Sometimes they were sympathetic; most of the time they were not.

'What does it matter?' said a stork at one end of the world. 'We each have our own talents.'

'Don't take on so,' said a kiwi at the other. 'Look at me, I can't even fly!'

'Give it up,' said a puffin. 'Be thankful for what you have already.'

'Yeah!' said a thrush, 'haven't you got enough?'

The squirlybird was tempted to say he deserved more than enough, but thought that that was perhaps too selfish and held his tongue. Then he heard again the mockingbird's cruel laugh and remembered the sweet melody from even the tiniest, dullest looking songbird and decided that no, he absolutely did deserve it and he would find the secret to singing even if it killed him.

'But why?' asked a swallow. 'When your beauty, your storytelling, your aeronautical skills are supreme, the envy of all – well, almost all – why do you need to sing?'

'Because without that I am incomplete,' was now always his answer. 'How can I be the very best, the most admired bird in creation if I can't sing?'

Finally, he consulted an owl who was reputed to be the wisest on the planet. But if he expected advice or encouragement, he was sadly mistaken. 'Face it, chum,' said the owl, after listening to his dismal efforts and then peering down his throat. 'You don't have the wherewithal.'

'The what?'

'The tackle, the bits necessary for a goodly warble. Some of us have it, most of us don't. Consider the...' And here the owl reeled off a string of names of birds hopelessly deficient in the music-making department. 'Then of course,' he continued, 'there's me. Can't sing a note. Couldn't manage it even if my life depended on it. But does that make me less of a bird? Does it diminish my wisdom? Not one jot! And am I disheartened? Am I dispirited? Am I–?'

'Oh, shut up!' said the squirlybird crossly and flew off, more depressed but more determined than ever.

'Give us a break!' you might have been saying ever since this story began. 'If this bird is so marvellous, how come we've never heard of it?' Or, 'Pull the other one! There's no such thing as a squirlybird!' And you're right. There is no such bird – not now, but there was once a very long time ago.

And here begins the saddest part, for just as *he* existed, the first and last of his remarkable kind, so too did a *she* squirlybird exist, the first and last of her kind. She was not as fast or as colourful or as extraordinary as him. She couldn't sing either (though, oddly, any noise she made was marginally better than his croaks and honks), but she hardly cared.

The 'she' squirlybird had always known about the 'he'. With a creature so wonderful and so famous how could she not? But she was free-spirited, and like him, proud and stubborn; she valued her independence. Even more, she valued her peace and quiet. Not for her his showy, flamboyant ways. In fact, she rather disliked him and took every opportunity to avoid him. Then she heard about his humiliation, and something stirred within her. She also admitted that perhaps it was time to play her part, for in nature, even with all its versatility, it still takes two to make a third, a fourth, and so on. With this in mind, she set aside her dislike, and now as he criss-crossed the globe in search of the secret of singing so she did the same in search of him. But always when she got to where he should have been, he wasn't anymore. Days, weeks, months passed without success. She had almost given up all hope of ever finding him until one morning, there he was.

By now she was exhausted, as thin as a twig and even less attractive. Indeed, she was in such a feeble state that he scarcely recognized her as a bird, let alone his own kind. Summoning her remaining strength, she fluffed up her feathers in an attempt to interest him, opened her mouth... and expired on the spot. As for him, he looked down at the wizened scrap of a corpse, almost felt sad, but then with his mind intent on his elusive goal flew off.

Given enough time, would he have found what he was seeking? Hard to say. Besides, time was against him, for he, too, was growing desperately weary. All that flying and searching, all that disappointment, had taken its toll. Gradually the shine and colour faded from his feathers and the determination waned until finally he was nothing more than a shell. With his last breath he squawked a horrible squawk and plummeted senseless to the ground.

And that's why the magnificent squirlybird is seen and heard no more; in fact, hardly ever mentioned. Besides, maybe it's just not done in nature for any creature – man, beast or bird – to have it all.

Going Up, Going Down, Going Out

In a town to the north west of London there was until quite recently a rather odd hotel. Built in the mid 1930s, the hotel was neither small nor grand, and as countless buildings of that era go it had little in particular to recommend it – apart, that is, from two exceptional features: the lifts that carried the guests and staff from one of its seven floors to another.

The hotel was built as an investment by an entrepreneurial northerner whose business had flourished so successfully that he found himself with more money than he knew how to spend. Feeling unappreciated in his local world, Hector (for that was the northerner's name) decided to move south. At that time, the Metropolitan Railway was extending its services beyond London into the leafy county of Buckinghamshire, and it was forecast that this would bring a new prosperity to some of the towns in the area.

'Just the place for a smart hotel,' said Hector to his wife, stabbing the map where a new station on the line was shortly to open. 'Mark my words,' he added, 'they'll be thronging there in no time.' His wife was not so sure, and though she voiced a few objections (she knew better than to argue) he bought a plot of land, demolished the coaching inn that had stood on it for more than two centuries, and hired an up-and-coming architect from Chicago.

Besides being an imaginative fellow, Clifton J. Wilbro (for that was the architect's name) had three passions which he liked to incorporate in whatever he was working on: one of the three was geometric designs, another was elevators.

'You mean lifts,' said Hector, when he and Wilbro first met to talk about the possibilities. 'That's what *we* call them, doubtless for the very good reason that they lift people from one floor to another.' It's only fair to state here that Hector had little sense of humour at the best of times, and certainly none at all when it came to his money; having earned it the hard way, he was determined to make it difficult to part with.

'Ditto with elevators,' Wilbro said cheerfully.

'Eh?'

'Do they not elevate people?'

Hector didn't care for fancy words. 'Doubtless they do,' he replied, 'but it's my hotel and as far as I'm concerned they're lifts.'

'Okay,' laughed Wilbro, before breaking into song: 'You say lift, I say elevator. Let's call the whole thing off!'

'Oh! No need for that, surely?' said Hector, on whom the allusion was completely lost.

Somewhat disheartened by the man's attitude but eager to secure the contract Wilbro moved on to other design matters and the subject of lifts was forgotten. However, when the two met a few months later to study the preliminary plans it resurfaced.

'These here,' said Hector, tapping a pair of sketches. 'What are they?'

'The elev– the lifts,' said Wilbro. His sketches for the exterior of the lifts, suggested by some he had noted in New York, were particularly colourful and detailed; the sketches for the two interiors even more so. He had little hope of their being accepted, but as a typical 'nothing venture nothing gain' sort of fellow he thought he would try. If Hector turned them down he could always use the idea somewhere else.

'Bit fancy, wouldn't you say?' asked Hector. 'Costly too, by the look of 'em.'

'But unique,' said Wilbro. 'They'll be an asset; they'll help to define your hotel, to 'lift it' (pun intended) from the ordinary to the exceptional. Besides, you said you liked brass.'

'Aye, I did. And you've certainly not stinted there,' agreed Hector, who had always had a soft spot for highly-polished metals. And then, with almost a smile: 'It'll take some cleaning.'

'Is that a yes?'

'I reckon it is, lad. Mind you, if I'm going to spend

that much you'd better make 'em special.'

And Clifton J. Wilbro did 'make 'em special', so special in fact that while the Chalfont (for that was the hotel's name) was admired for its bold and innovative designs when it opened some eleven months later, no features were more talked about and written about than the lifts. Their reputation spread far and wide, and as Hector had once predicted people thronged to the hotel. Sadly, their thronging was not always to stay in the hotel's rooms, to eat in the hotel's restaurant or even to drink in the hotel's bar. More often than not it was solely to ride up and down in the two lifts. Eventually, Hector the businessman (or hotelier as he now preferred to be known) got wise to their enjoyment and put a stop to it.

I mentioned earlier that Wilbro had three passions. He had already indulged two of them: geometric designs and elevators. To the mix he now added his third passion, Hollywood musicals, by naming the lifts 'Fred' and 'Ginger' after two movie stars who were particularly famous at that time for their singing and dancing. Odd names for lifts? Certainly! And of course they didn't dance or sing – that would be silly even for this story – but the designs gave them a style and flair that was unusual in that part of the country.

For five years the Chalfont did reasonably well, almost as well as Hector had predicted. Then a world war intervened and somehow the hotel – popular with a variety of servicemen and women – did even better.

Throughout the long, turbulent years of the war, Fred and Ginger continued to play their part, until an enemy bomb intended for a nearby factory damaged one side of the hotel. Although Fred was not directly involved, and indeed continued to remain almost fully functional, he was never quite the same again.

When the hotel first opened the lifts were operated by a team of liftboys. Smartly uniformed with white gloves and pillbox caps (also designed by Wilbro), they would convey guests and luggage to whichever floor was requested. A few years after the war, Hector found the boys to be an unnecessary expense and replaced them with a self-operated system. While this was more convenient for the guests it was not always pleasant for Fred and Ginger as they felt their buttons jabbed impatiently, sometimes twice or even three or more times.

'Why their impatience makes them think I'll move any faster beats me,' sighed Ginger, 'but still they do it.'

To her, the guests were a constant mystery. 'I just don't understand them,' she said to Fred one night (in the still of the night while stationary on the ground floor the two liked to swap stories about the day's goings on).

'Don't try to understand them,' said Fred philosophically. 'I don't. If they want to go to this floor or that, I take them, as I'm supposed to do.'

'Of course,' Ginger agreed. 'But you must admit that their behaviour is sometimes very odd.'

'Very,' said Fred.

It wasn't just their behaviour she didn't understand,

it was their many different languages and accents. It's a well-known fact that walls have ears, and this was certainly true in a small space such as that in Fred and Ginger. One of their delights was to hear all the different voices – some harsh and angry, others soft and musical. Over the years she and Fred had picked up quite a vocabulary. And favourites, too. With Fred it was Italians. With Ginger, perhaps because of Wilbro and his background, it was Americans; not the very loud or the very heavy ones (five or six of them and she really felt the strain), but the quieter ones who admired her and called her 'elevator', a word which seemed to her so much finer than the dull and monosyllabic 'lift'.

'I'm an elevator,' she said proudly. 'I elevate people.' She, in particular, loved elevating people, transporting them and their luggage from floor to floor. 'Such a valuable service I perform.'

Although she and Fred were almost identical, on closer inspection it could be seen by the most observant that Wilbro had lavished slightly more care and attention on her – probably because he was more in love with her screen image than he was with Fred's. Whether the guests were aware of this difference or not, she was always the preferred one; while Fred was enjoyed, Ginger was adored. Or so she liked to feel. Scarcely a day went by when she didn't thank Hector for his money and sing Clifton J. Wilbro's praises for her loveliness.

And then of course there was Winston. Before the hotel's grand opening, Hector had brought down from the north a married couple: Betty to keep a stern eye on the housekeeping, her husband Albert to deal with odd jobs or to supervise others dealing with odd jobs. The arrangement worked well for more than 30 years until the work became too much for them, at which time they retired to a bungalow on the South Coast and their son Winston took over.

Born in the hotel the night the stray bomb fell, young Winston grew to learn every inch of the hotel, every nook and cranny (in Wilbro's quirky design there were a few), its good points and its bad ones (a few of those, too). While not a master in all aspects of his various duties, Winston took great pride in them. From the word go his very favourite task was to keep Fred and Ginger smart and polished. This he did every morning and evening, and sometimes in-between if needed.

And that's when they had the conversations: one-sided conversations, of course, because although Winston could talk to Fred and Ginger, being 'things' they couldn't talk back (a sad fact of nature). The best of these took place after midnight when Winston came to polish away the day's fingerprints. Always as he polished he talked to them, told them what was going on with the guests and with the staff, and sometimes with the world beyond the hotel. And they listened with keen interest.

Every so often he'd come by unexpectedly to chat about a new guest. 'Do you know who that was?' or even, 'You'll never guess who you've just taken up to the bridal suite!' (Yes, there was a bridal suite; a penthouse, too. Initially, Hector had refused both. 'New-fangled exclusivities!' he called them, until Wilbro assured him – correctly – of the extra revenue, after which Hector was delighted.) Ginger, especially, loved these moments: the sound of Winston's voice, the tidbits of news.

Fred and Ginger often had news of their own. As you read earlier, they found the behaviour of some of the guests very odd. For Ginger, the more sensitive of the two, this could be disturbing, and there were moments when she felt very ill-used. More than once a young couple had stopped the lift between floors to engage in passionate acts, and Ginger would cry out 'Get a room!' Not that they took any notice, of course. Occasionally, events necessitated an 'Out of Order' notice on her doors, such as the time when the rather wild supporters of a visiting football team decided to celebrate by smearing her walls with slogans that shocked even Winston.

Big parties could be a problem, too: especially those on New Year's Eve, as people became sillier and louder and more reckless as the night wore on. The same was even more true of stag nights and hen parties (what on earth were they? she wondered when she first heard the terms; she soon discovered and very much wished she hadn't). By far the worst was when– but no, the memory of that was too appalling. There are some things no self-respecting elevator should ever suffer. She liked a party as much as anyone, but there are limits.

By contrast, there were pleasant, heartwarming experiences. Sometimes, in the harsh winter months, there were power cuts in the town and in the hotel. When that happened Ginger might find herself stuck fast between one floor and another. On one such occasion a mother and her two small children were trapped for more than an hour. They were on the verge of becoming really quite distressed until another occupant at the time, an old gentleman with a kindly voice, enthralled the children with a story about a princess locked in a tower by a wicked witch. Every day the tower grew taller and taller until it began to disappear into the clouds. And then one night a mighty eagle flew in through the window. But was the eagle a handsome prince come to rescue her or the wicked wit–? Sadly, for Ginger, the power came back on just at that moment so she never did learn the end of the story.

A much happier ending came just a few weeks later while carrying a young woman and her husband. The woman had gone into labour sooner than expected and the couple were on their way to the hospital. But halfway to the ground floor the power went again and they were stranded. By the time the fire brigade arrived to open the doors (fortunately, they didn't need to force them) she had given birth to a baby girl. And what did she call her? Ginger, which of course pleased Ginger no end.

All in all, it was a good life. So it had been from the start. And so they thought it would continue forever. But nothing is forever. After nearly five decades of owning and running the hotel Hector died. A few months later his wife followed him. Then there came in short succession a series of proprietors, each one less attentive to the hotel's needs than the one before. Gradually that lack of attention began to show in the paint and plaster and in the fixtures and fittings. Then one morning, almost 60 years to the day since the Chalfont's grand opening some estate agents arrived. They took measurements throughout the hotel, even in Fred and Ginger. That should have told her something. The following day a photographer came and clicked away. This was nothing new. Ginger had been photographed countless times before, together with admiring tourists and visitors, and sometimes with old friends who posed inside and outside the lift and stroked the well-polished brass and bronze. But this photographer was different. No admiring photos, just cold, matter-of-fact ones. That, too, should have told her something.

A few days later Winston came and his voice sounded very different. First he talked to Fred, so quietly that Ginger couldn't catch what he was saying. Eventually he moved across the hall.

'Well, princess…' As he often began in this way, she was expecting some gossip. Instead he surprised her: 'Looks like the end of us. Me, and you too.'

'What's he saying?' thought Ginger.

'I've had a word with Fred,' he continued. 'I've not told him everything. Don't want to upset him. There'll be enough of that later. Don't know yet what's in store for you. They're still undecided. There's been some talk of a museum. You'd like that, wouldn't you?'

A museum! Ginger had heard of museums, and no, she didn't think she'd like that one bit. To be stuck in one place and stared at and photographed and… On the other hand, she enjoyed being photographed and admired, so perhaps it mightn't be so bad. She'd be respected, too; as she deserved. No more kids with their sticky fingers, no more impatient lovers with their rather dreadful habits, no more hen parties and stag nights. 'Yes, that might suit me very well.'

'That might suit you very well,' said Winston, as if reading her thoughts. 'But as I say, there's nothing settled at the moment. Except for poor old Fred.'

'There he goes again,' thought Ginger. 'What does he mean about Fred?' Oh, if only she could ask him questions!

'As for me,' sighed Winston, 'it's my last day. There's no need for me anymore. No need! Can you believe it after all these years? Well, I've got some packing to do. But I just wanted to say it's been a real pleasure looking after you both. An honour, too. I'm only sorry it has to end like this. Goodbye, old friend,' he said, and a moment later he was gone.

'Wait!' cried Ginger, 'what are you talking about?'

After that, nothing very much happened for a day or two, or it could have been a week or two. The hotel was closed and the building that had been so lively for so long was now cold and empty. But a while later two workmen arrived. They went to Fred and began banging and drilling and hammering, and none too gently either. She could hear him complaining. At first Ginger thought the workmen were mending something. Maintenance, that was the word. This had happened a number of times over the years, as was only natural: parts wore out, they got replaced. They both accepted that and welcomed it, especially if it made for smoother running. For the most part *she* had stayed fairly intact. Not so poor Fred who seemed to suffer one complication after another. In the last few months he had started creaking and groaning quite alarmingly, so clearly a bit of maintenance was needed. But this was no maintenance, this was dismantling: they were taking Fred apart bit by bit!

Later that day three sharp-suited, sharp-voiced businessmen stepped in and jabbed the button for the top floor, not once or twice but three times. Oh, how Ginger wished at that point not to move, but efficient as ever she took them up. As she rose she could hardly believe what she heard: words like 'sold', 'vacant plot', 'prime site', 'fit for development', and worst of all 'available for scrap'.

"Available for scrap"?' she cried angrily.

All through that night she thought of the years that had passed, of Winston and Fred, of the chats and the polish, and most of all of her loveliness, and slowly her anger turned to bitterness and her bitterness to hate. For Ginger, these were very new feelings, very strange feelings, and she didn't know how to control them, or even if she wanted to. And then she thought again of poor old Fred now broken up and taken away in bits and pieces to be sold as scrap, and how it was probably her turn next. 'And after all I've done for them,' she fumed. 'No, I will not be scrap. I will NOT be scrap!'

By the morning she'd made up her mind. 'If I'm going, I'm taking them with me. I'll make them regret they ever treated me in such a way!' But though she was now burning with revenge, she had as yet no clear plan how to take it. She was on the ground floor. The power was off. She was going nowhere! And then it happened, the chance she needed. Just as the two men from the day before clattered in with their heavy boxes of tools to begin work on her, another man rushed in.

'I'm not too late then!' he said breathlessly.

'Too late?' said one of the workmen.

'Just need to get some photos of the view from the roof, before they start with the wrecking ball,' said the new arrival. Ginger recognized his voice as that of one of the businessmen from the previous day. 'So, top floor.'

'Can't do that, mate, the power's off,' said the first workman. 'You'll have to take the stairs.'

'You can turn it back on, can't you? This won't take long.'

'Well…' the first workman began to say.

'What's this to be then?' said the second. 'Car park, supermarket, office block?'

'As long I get the right price for the site,' said the businessman, 'it can stay a hole in the ground for all I care.'

'The right price, eh?' said the second workman.

'Okay. Give us a tenner, and we'll take you.'

'Ten pounds!'

'Each,' he said. 'Or you know where the stairs are.'

Grudgingly the businessman agreed. The money changed hands, the power was restored, the button for the top floor was jabbed (three times), and the doors closed.

'Ha!' screamed Ginger. 'I've got you now! I'll give you a ride you'll remember for the rest of your lives, if you remember anything at all!'

And as she sped to the top she heaved and groaned and juddered and shuddered with all her might till the cables wailed in distress and the very nuts and bolts rattled themselves loose. And in her final moments – though no one could hear above the frightful din – she shrieked: 'this is for Winston, this is for Fred, and this is for Meeee!'

Some hours later in a senior partner's office on the 53rd floor of a building in Chicago the intercom buzzed.

'Potter, calling from London,' said the senior partner's secretary.

'Put him on,' said the senior partner, and when he was on: 'Potter! How's it going over there?'

'Well, sir,' replied a rather nervous Potter. 'That lift you were interested in, the 1930s one at the Chalfont Hotel?'

'Ginger? What about her?'

'Did you have any particular plans for it?'

'You bet. She's the centrepiece for a new museum right here. They'll be shipping her any day now.'

There was a sharp intake of breath from London.

'There a problem with that?' asked Chicago.

'There's been a bit of an accident. Rather a serious one. You see...'

As the senior partner listened to the tale of destruction, of the broken, mangled remains far away in a small town to the north west of London, his face fell and he covered his eyes with his hand.

Finally he asked, 'And there's nothing left?'

'There's the scrap, of course,' said Potter. 'But I'm afraid there's also—'

Chicago didn't wait for the rest. He ended the call, put down the phone and from his desk took up a framed colour photo. Though faded it showed clearly a young man beaming proudly beside Ginger, the first and finest of all his elevators. 'What a waste,' said Clifton J. Wilbro III sadly. 'What a waste.'

The Pixie's Quest

It had been a long week for the pixie. Although one of the winged variety he preferred to keep his feet firmly on the ground, and since setting off from his home so many miles away he had trudged and tramped through wind, rain and even snow. Now he was tired, hungry, and more than a little dirty. More significantly, he was bored. The whole point of leaving his comfortable space with his pixie friends and relations was to experience life, to see the big wide world he'd heard so much about (mostly from pixies who had heard stories only from pixies who had themselves heard the stories only from other pixies, who had probably never travelled further than the forest at the edge of the lake). But up to this point in his quest for an exciting life he'd seen little of any interest, and now in the middle of the seventh day he was deeply disappointed. He was also disgruntled, and if you know anything about pixies you'll know that a disgruntled one is a must to avoid.

He was on the verge of chucking it in and returning home, when a rustling close by caught his attention. Crouching down, he spied a something shambling through the undergrowth. Such an odd looking something it was, and one that he'd certainly never seen before. To get a better view he crept nearer and nearer, and then – not being the most observant of pixies – he tripped on the root of a tree and flew headlong into the something's backside.

'Oh me, oh my!' he cried (though not nearly so politely, as you'd discover often in this tale if it weren't for careful editing, for the pixie was certainly no novice in the foul language department; bump into him on a bad day and you'd find the air very blue). 'Oh, me!' he cried again as he felt sharp bits sticking into places where no bits should ever stick. 'What the blinkin' hell's this?'

'It's to stop people like you hitching a ride without so much as a by your leave is what it is,' said the something tetchily.

'I'm not a people, I'm a pixie,' he complained.

'Then you should know better.'

'Ah, you're probably right,' said the pixie, nursing various parts of his body. 'Trouble is, I don't really know nothing, which is why–'

'Anything,' the something interrupted (thinking, 'that's all I need, an illiterate').

'Eh?' said the pixie.

'I don't really know anything,' the something insisted.

'You don't? Oh, that's a bummer,' said the pixie. 'I was hoping you would. You see, the whole point of–'

'No, no, no! You can't say "I don't know nothing", that's a double negative and most incorrect.'

'Is it?'

'You need to say "I don't know anything",' continued the something, whose father had been a stickler for grammatical niceties and suchlike.

'Oh, I see,' said the pixie (who didn't). More puzzled than usual, he stared at the odd-looking something covered in sharp prickly spines. 'Excuse me for asking,' he said, 'but what are you?'

The something had never been asked such a question before and it took him a minute or so to find an answer. 'I'm me,' he said at last.

'Of course, yeah,' agreed the pixie, 'but what type of "me"? For example, I'm also "me" and I'm a pixie.'

'Aaaah, if that's what you're asking then I'm a porcupine. Have you never seen one before?'

The pixie was about to confess that he hadn't then changed his mind and said instead: 'Of course! But clearly you've never seen a pixie before so allow me to introduce meself.' And he did, taking the opportunity to tell of his journey so far, together with some rather extravagant embellishments. The porcupine listened to this silly chatter for a while and then, unimpressed, set off for a quieter, cooler spot.

The pixie was not used to being ignored. 'Oh!' he said, again none too politely, then decided that perhaps the porcupine was hard of hearing. With this in mind he followed him and began to tell his story again, but more loudly.

'This is all very well,' yawned the porcupine after

the first minute, 'and I don't wish to be rude but I'm really not interested.'

The pixie was quite taken aback. How could anyone not be fascinated in such details as he had to tell? 'Well,' he said, 'never let it be said I can't take a hint. On the other hand, if you're certain you're not interested...?'

'Quite,' the porcupine replied, and to prove it he rolled himself into a sort of a ball and began snoring.

The pixie stood there, unsure whether to stay or go. After a while he came to the conclusion that the porcupine was not going to emerge anytime soon. 'Please yourself,' he muttered huffily and went off to explore.

Sad to say, there wasn't much to explore in the immediate vicinity, and after the pixie found himself back at the same boring clump of bushes three times in a row, he decided that the next day he would continue on his quest for excitement in the big wide world.

Oddly, it was the porcupine who changed his mind. The pixie had just settled down for a good night's sleep when he felt a nudge.

'It's probably none of my business,' said the porcupine, 'but as you're new to these parts it's only fair to warn you about sleeping here.'

True to character, the pixie was immediately on the defensive. 'What's it to you?' he cried, springing up with fists clenched. 'These your own private bushes, are they?'

'Not at all,' said the porcupine. 'But if you do sleep here you'll wake up with an awful rash. It's the sap from that tree. It drips down overnight and the result can be most unpleasant.'

'Oh,' said the pixie, calming down. 'That's kind of you. I appreciate it.'

'Don't mention it,' said the porcupine. He started to move away then turned back. 'I can show you a better place. If you like?'

'Well, yeah!' said the pixie.

Not much used to conversation, the porcupine moved away, and the pixie followed. After they'd walked in silence for a while, the porcupine stopped by a very different tree. 'Here's as good a place as any for the night,' he said. 'You'll be quite comfortable here.' And without another word he ambled off into the undergrowth.

'Oh, yeah... thanks. Goodnight!' the pixie called, and for the first time that day he smiled. 'Quite a pleasant bloke really,' he said to himself. 'Maybe I'll stick around and get to know him better.' Then he settled himself under the tree and went to sleep.

Over the next few days the pixie got to know the porcupine very well, or as well as could be expected with someone who not only didn't seem to do much or know much, but showed absolutely no inclination to want to do much or know much. But why should he? Solitary by nature, he was not used to company, especially talkative company. A creature of quiet routine, he liked nothing better than a leisurely snuffle in the undergrowth in the hope of finding something mildly interesting: 'mildly' being the important word, for he was not given to excitement. On the rare occasions when his snuffling did turn up something mildly interesting his day was made. On the other hand, if he found nothing at all then that too was a good result, meaning as it did that statistically he had an even greater chance of a mildly interesting discovery in the days to come. An odd way of thinking perhaps (if he thought about it at all, which he didn't), but it suited him. Besides, he would say to himself, could there be anything more to life?

This lack of curiosity exasperated the pixie. He couldn't understand how the porcupine could bear to live such a dull, uneventful existence. 'Don't you ever wonder what's out there?' he asked one morning.

'What's out where?' replied the porcupine, stumped, and at the same time thinking what a silly question.

'Out there in the big wide world, way past these trees and bushes, way beyond this valley even.'

'Why? What's the point?' answered the porcupine.

'But think of the adventures to be had. Such fun! And such riches!'

'Riches? What's that?' asked the porcupine, who had never heard the word before and so had no idea what it could mean.

Now it was the pixie's turn to be stumped. He had heard the word 'riches' before, but hadn't the vaguest notion what it meant. 'Well, it's... it's...' he struggled, 'hard to explain. It's like when something strange happens... something so completely unexpected... dangerous perhaps, but so rewarding.'

'Dangerous': another word the porcupine had never heard before. In his sheltered, comfy life there was no danger, and so the word was meaningless. Even so, it made him feel uneasy and he shivered. 'Oh, I'm not sure I would like that. In fact, I don't think I would like it at all.'

'Wouldn't it be exciting?'

'I can't see why,' said the porcupine.

'But think of what you're missing!'

'Missing? The sun comes up, the sun goes down. What else is there?'

'That's... that's... Oh, I give up!' cried the pixie. And he did. Never one to refuse a challenge, however, later that evening he tried again. 'Up there,' he said, pointing to the sky which, apart from the twinkling stars, was now inky black with darkness. 'What do you see?'

The porcupine, whose sight was poor at the best of times, squinted at the vast beyond. 'What do I see? Nothing. It's too dark.'

'All right, think of during the day. When you look up into the sky, what do you see?'

'Another silly question,' thought the porcupine, then replied: 'Nothing, it's just sky. Blue rather than black, I grant you, but still just sky.'

'Oh!' cried the pixie in frustration. 'Have you no soul? No imagination? To think of all those wonders completely wasted on you!'

Matters came to a head just over a week after they had first met. For days, the pixie had been trying to find some topic that would rouse the porcupine's curiosity. He talked about this, he talked about that, about subjects he knew, and quite a few of which he was woefully ignorant (a lack of knowledge had never stopped him before and he saw no reason to hold back now). By the evening, overwhelmed by the torrent, the porcupine could stand it no longer.

'You do talk the most awful rot!' he said, stamping his feet.

'Rot?'

'Rot!' repeated the porcupine. 'I might not have travelled and lived an exciting life like you, but that doesn't mean I'm stupid.'

'Oh,' the pixie replied, and again: 'Oh.' He knew perfectly – no one better – that the tales he told were often exaggerated and wildly economical with the truth. But he had always supposed that if nothing else he was entertaining, and for that surely he could be forgiven. Feeling very hurt he pulled himself up to his utmost height and asked in a rather pompous voice: 'Is there anything in particular that has brought you to this conclusion, unfair and unsubstantiated as it may be?'

The porcupine considered the question for a moment, and having guessed the gist of it he replied: 'All of it.'

'All of it? But that's im- impossible!' the pixie stammered.

'You talk and talk and talk and talk! Prattling on and on about nothing much in particular without even drawing breath. I'm amazed you don't keel over from exhaustion.'

For the pixie, who prided himself on his conversational skills, this accusation was especially wounding. 'I have never ever talked about nothing much in particular,' he sniffed defensively.

'It's not as if you say anything of interest,' continued the porcupine.

For the pixie this was the last straw. 'Not of interest?' he snorted. 'Right, that's it. I shall be leaving in the morning!'

'Good!' said the porcupine. And they parted that night on very bad terms.

But again the porcupine changed the pixie's mind. Very unusually that night the porcupine was restless, sleepless. He did look up into the sky, and though he still couldn't see anything he began to wonder if – as the pixie claimed – there could be something more out there. Fragments of the pixie's nonsense swirled around his mind and some of them struck a chord. Of course, he didn't believe a fraction of what he'd heard, but he had to admit that he'd rather enjoyed his days since the pixie arrived.

The next morning the pixie awoke with a start to find two eyes staring down at him. 'What! What's happened?' he cried.

'Tell me more,' said the porcupine. And, never one to hold a grudge, the pixie told him more. And the more the porcupine heard (even though much of it was still nonsense), the more he looked forward to spending time with the pixie.

They started taking walks together, venturing further into unknown areas. Truth to tell, these walks for the pixie were somewhat tedious as the porcupine could move only at a rather slow speed, but they gave the opportunity for even more talk.

One day, when they had walked farther than usual, they came to a lake. Fringed with trees, the cool clear water sparkled invitingly in the bright sun.

'Perfect!' cried the pixie, and began stripping off his clothes.

The porcupine was astonished. 'What are you doing?'

'Going for a swim, of course!'

'A what?'

'A swim! You know, splash splash!'

'In there?'

'What better place?' And without another word, he clambered up a tree, ran along a high branch, swung himself off and dived in.

The porcupine had never seen such antics. 'How do you do that?' he gasped.

'Oh, it's easy! Come on, I'll show you.'

'Me? Certainly not!'

Over the days that followed they visited the lake again and again, and though the pixie never managed to persuade the porcupine to take the plunge he did succeed in getting him to perch on the edge and wiggle his feet in the crystal clear water.

'There, doesn't that feel good?'

'Well,' said the porcupine, 'it does have a certain something to recommend it.'

'So think how much better you'll enjoy it with the rest of you.'

'The rest of me? I couldn't possibly,' the porcupine protested. 'For one thing, I should be all wet.'

'But it's fun!'

'Yes,' the porcupine agreed happily. 'It does look like fun.'

There was a lull in the conversation as they both thought about this, and then suddenly the pixie said: 'Look, mate. You and me, chalk and cheese!'

'I don't know what that is.'

'What, chalk and cheese? It's your figure of speech, innit?'

The porcupine looked blank, and the pixie explained: 'Well, cheese is something you eat − and very nice, thank you − and chalk isn't.'

'I still don't understand.'

'What I'm trying to say is that you and me, we're different; very different. Which is a good thing, innit?'

'Is it?'

'I should say so! Makes it all so much more interesting. So, I've been thinking: why don't you come with me?'

'Come with you? Where?'

'On my travels! To see things you've never seen before, do things you've never done before!'

'But we don't know what we might find... or what might find us!'

'Ah, so you have got an imagination!'

'Not really,' replied the porcupine. 'And anyway, what's the point?'

'Oh, you and your "what's the point?" all the time! You might as well ask what's the point of a porcupine? Or, for that matter, a pixie?'

'Good question,' said the porcupine. 'What *is* the point of a pixie?'

This question had never occurred to the pixie, but now that it had he hardly dared consider an answer. What if there wasn't any point?

Curiously, the porcupine was at last beginning to consider the opposite: what if the pixie were right and there was a point to it all? For one brief and delightful moment he saw himself travelling the world and–

'Well,' said the pixie, interrupting the porcupine's thought, 'perhaps there isn't a point to you, me, or anything at all, here or anywhere else. But who cares so long as it's fun, interesting, exciting? Besides,' he continued, 'it's so much better if one does it with a friend.'

'What's a friend?'

'What's a–?' the pixie began. He almost snorted at such ignorance but then realised that perhaps the porcupine had never had one. Then he had to admit to himself that although he had often thought about his pixie friends he couldn't in all honesty name a single *real* one, certainly not one with whom he'd shared so much as he'd shared with the porcupine. He tried to explain some of this and when he saw a glimmer of understanding in the porcupine's eyes he added: 'How about it then? Coming with me?'

'Yes, I could,' said the porcupine, warming to the idea. But then he made a suggestion that quite tempted the pixie: 'Or you could stay here.'

That night they were both sleepless as they considered the options: for the pixie, a life of peace and comfort with his new friend in which he could prattle away to his heart's content about adventures past and ones he could only imagine; for the porcupine, a journey into the unknown.

By the morning their decision was made.

'Well then,' said the pixie as he finished packing his few belongings. 'I'll be off.'

'Right.'

'Cheerio.'

'Right.'

'And you're sure you won't join me?'

'Quite.'

'It doesn't have to be today. I could easily go tomorrow.'

This time, no response. The porcupine stared hard at the ground, which of course was dreadfully frustrating for the pixie. He edged forward a pace or two. 'Ta-ta then. I'm really going,' he said. The porcupine's sharp spines quivered and he continued to stare at the ground. When finally he looked up, he was alone.

He never saw the pixie again. Occasionally he would stop his snuffling, peer up into the vast, endless sky and wonder if the little chap ever found the adventures he was seeking. Even less occasionally he wondered if he shouldn't have gone with him; but almost as soon as that thought entered his mind he pushed it out, for it always made him rather sad, and not a little ashamed that he hadn't.

The Wasp and the Olive Tree

There was not so long ago and not so far from here an olive tree. As olive trees go it was not large, nor was it very handsome or even very healthy, but there was about it a certain something, and one afternoon towards the end of summer this certain something caught the attention of a young wasp. It was by then late afternoon, and though the sun still peeped brightly between the clouds, the wind was beginning to cool the air: a reminder of the coming season of autumn.

The wasp, ZX23798KQ74 (2nd class), or ZX74 for short, was on his way home after a long trip's foraging. Being young and inexperienced in the length of days and journeys and feeling rather tired, he decided to rest awhile. He was wondering where to set down when he spied the tree. Standing in the middle of a meadow it was unlike any he'd seen before. The leaves were a sort of green on top and a sort of silvery grey underneath.

'Hmmm,' said ZX74 who had a curious mind. 'That looks unusual. Worth a visit.' And so saying, down he flew. The past few weeks had been difficult and things had happened that troubled him, but what he found as he alighted on the tree was a sense of peace and calm. It almost made him forget that sooner or later he would have to return to the colony.

As you know, wasps are not noted for their bonhomie; in fact, quite the opposite. They're an aggressive lot, even to each other. For most of his young life ZX74 had not been aware of this. Because he had never known anything else the behaviour of his fellow wasps seemed quite normal, and so it might have continued to seem had it not been for 'the challenge' a few weeks earlier.

It's probably a little known fact that although wasps are officially allotted a series of numbers and letters (hence ZX23798KQ74), one or two of the more individual characters attract nicknames, usually due to some idiosyncrasy in their manner. As often happens with such names, most of them (such as Dopey or Sticky) are sillier than others, but within this particular colony there were one or two who acquired theirs for reasons of daring or foolhardiness. An example of the latter was Dippy, so called for his habit of dipping his body in a most unwasplike way just before homing in for the sting. Needless to say, this peculiar time-wasting trait soon cost him his life. A prime example of the former... well, you'll learn about him very shortly. Suffice it to say, he already had quite a reputation as a rogue and a bully. (Sadly, there's always one.)

It happened that a council of elderly wasps

were meeting to discuss certain rather alarming developments between their colony and a neighbouring one when the rogue burst in.

'I got one! I got one, so I did!' he cried.

The seniors eyed him coldly. Even in a wasps' nest there are good manners and bad manners, and to interrupt in this way was certainly bad manners.

'You got one what?' the principal elder asked frostily.

'One of the two-legs,' cried the young rogue with glee. 'She was just about to put a... a... something in her mouth and I timed it to perfection!' Boasting was appreciated even less than interrupting, but he was so full of himself and his adventure that he scarcely noticed the rather embarrassed if not hostile silence.

'That, no doubt, was very clever of you,' said the elder, 'but I really think–' The elder would have continued with a stern rebuke but the rogue was determined to have his moment of glory.

'No, no, no!' he went on regardless. 'I got her on the lip, and not on the outer but on the inner! Oh, how she howled!'

'On the inner lip, you say?'

'You betcha!' he said, brimming with confidence.

'Well... that is certainly something,' agreed the council. Undeniably impressed, they forgave the rogue his interruption. To sting a two-legs on the inner lip or the tongue was quite a coup; one that many attempted but few achieved.

'Can anyone vouch for this remarkable achievement?' asked a sceptic (after all, it wouldn't be the first time a wasp had boasted untruthfully).

'I can!' said another young wasp, who had entered at about the same time. 'I was right behind. And what a sight to see. Go on!' he said to the rogue, 'show 'em your victory waggle.'

The rogue needed no prompting, and following a deft body flip he demonstrated a rapid waggling of his bottom. 'I do that,' he explained, 'then I'm straight in for the sting. They don't stand a chance!'

The sceptic was even more suspicious. 'You do this "victory waggle" before you sting? Isn't that rather presumptuous?'

'Not at all. When I choose my target, I never miss!'

A few of the older wasps were uncertain about such a manoeuvre and about the rogue's bragging, but the assembled others were impressed, and when one of them suggested the young hero be nicknamed Waggle the agreement was almost unanimous. But then came the challenge. Bursting with importance, and eager to build on his reputation, Waggle cried, 'And I challenge anyone in this colony to do as well as I have done!'

So began a competition to see who could sting the most; not just ordinary stings, mind you, but stings in really painful places. For a day or so the competition was reasonably lighthearted, but goaded by Waggle it soon became deadly serious as wasps both in that colony and in the next took up his challenge. So far,

only one had come close to emulating his success, but in the end the attempt proved just too close. When the two-legs opened her mouth to bite on a sausage the wasp dived inside and stung the inside of her lip. But he was too slow to get out in time: as his victim's teeth snapped shut in agony he was sliced in two.

'Oh, poor him! Good try but not good enough!' said Waggle, making no secret of his delight at his rival's demise.

For all his boasting Waggle himself had only managed two more successes, but neither of them on the lip or tongue. His most recent victory, as he never tired of telling them all, had been to send a couple of canoodling teenagers diving for cover into a pond. 'Such filthy, scummy water, too!' he cried. 'And I still got one of them on the ear, and the other on the nose! Oh, the thrill of it. The skill of it!'

'Not to mention the fun of it,' added one of his several supporters.

'Fun?' demanded Waggle. 'It's fun, yes! But so much more than that, it's sport. No,' he cried again, puffing himself up with importance, 'it's more than sport. It's artistry!'

Unlike most of the wasps in his colony ZX74 found Waggle's challenge disturbing. He couldn't understand how anyone could take such delight in causing pain to others even if they did have two legs. And as for stinging them on the lip or tongue, that was not his idea of a good time. In truth, he had tried. There was that incident with a family picnic (they had some delicious strawberry jam, and who even among the most insensitive of wasps can resist that?). But it was such a minor incident with only a little screaming and swatting. The reason for this was clear: his heart wasn't in it; he never really meant them any harm. 'Why is that fun, why is that sport?' he asked himself. And that of course was the difference between him and the others, and most especially between him and Waggle.

Foolishly, he mentioned his misgivings one day to his best friend (or to one he thought was his best friend, being too young to know that wasps don't have friends, best or otherwise). His words were reported back to the elders, and from then on he was considered an oddity, and whenever he passed by there were stares and glares and mutterings. Which is why, as he rested in the olive tree that first evening, he dreaded returning to the nest.

Eventually, he could put it off no longer.

Much to his surprise, no one made any comment, at least not to his face. The same was true the next evening and the one after that. During this time he spent many happy hours enjoying the peace and calm in the olive tree, basking in the sun on a leaf or, if it was raining, on the underside. And thinking, always thinking. And though he still dreaded going back he began to wonder if his remarks had been forgotten. Unknown to him, however, they hadn't. As the days passed and the competition became more fiercely contested his shameful score of not a single sting to his name did not go unnoticed. He began to be viewed by some of the colony as weird, by others as suspect, by other others as dangerous, and by all as an insult to the species. After a week of zero stings his failure was too blatant to ignore.

Returning home in a rather dreamy and thoughtful mood on the fourth evening after his discovery of the tree he collided with a wasp at the entrance.

'Oi! Watch yourself!' said the other, in that rather angry way that wasps tend to speak. Then he recognized ZX74. 'Oh, it's you, is it? I'm surprised you dare show your face!'

Something about his tone put ZX74 on alert.

'Did you think you could keep it a secret?' sneered the angry wasp. 'Word gets around, you know.'

'Am I in trouble?' he asked.

'You can say that again!'

'Oh,' said ZX74, unused to such remarks. 'Am I in trouble?'

'You get inside, and quick,' growled the angry wasp.

The chamber was packed. 'Ah, so kind of you to join us,' said the principal elder as ZX74 entered. 'We've been discussing your ridiculous behaviour.'

'Yes! Explain yourself!' cried an elderly wasp.

'But what have I done?' said ZX74.

'Nothing, and that's just the point!'

'The point, yes!' echoed the assembly.

'Not a single sting. Not one!'

'Ah, that,' said ZX74. 'Well er... there was almost one the other day.' And as he told them about the family picnic and the strawberry jam, their attitude towards him began to soften.

'So you got one?' the principal elder asked, delighted that he'd misunderstood the situation.

'Well, no.'

'So you didn't get one?' said the principal elder, now angrily as he realized he'd been misled.

'But you see,' said ZX74, 'I've been thinking about that, and I just wonder sometimes if perhaps we aren't... we aren't...'

'Aren't what?'

'Yes, out with it! What aren't we?'

'Er, too nasty,' said ZX74. 'I mean, nastier than we could be or should be.'

'Eh? What's the idiot babbling about?' asked one of the older, deafer wasps.

'What I mean is that couldn't we be... er,' ZX74 stumbled, hardly daring to speak the word, 'couldn't we... just for a change... be nice?'

This strange question drew a gasp from the assembly.

'Nice?' the elder roared (as much as a wasp can roar).

'Nice!' another roared, even louder so that the whole nest shook. 'We're not here to be nice, and the sooner you get that into your naive, do-goody head the better! You hear me?'

'You're absolutely right, of course. But…'

They all glared at him. ZX74 was not the most sensible of wasps, but now that he had broached the subject he felt he needed to continue. 'Why can't we be… we be…a bit more useful?'

'Useful?' demanded the elder.

'We are useful,' said a learned wasp. 'In our own way.'

'True, yes,' said ZX74. 'But couldn't we be *more* useful? More like bees, for example.'

At the mention of the B-word there was an even louder gasp.

'You're not seriously suggesting…?' spluttered one elderly wasp.

'Are you stupid or what?' Waggle hissed. 'You want us to be like those primitive things?'

'Primitive?' asked ZX74.

'Stands to reason,' replied another wasp. 'One sting, then goodnight bee.'

'Goodnight bee?' said ZX74, not understanding.

'They die, you fool,' said Waggle.

'He's right; only one sting, and that's them gone. Where's the sense in that?'

At this point ZX74 should of course have stayed silent. He didn't. 'But they do so much good!'

'Pah! Day after day, working, working, working from dawn till dusk,' said the learned one who probably knew more about the detested bees than all the others put together. 'And what have they to show for all that toil, I ask you?'

'Nothing!' cried a voice.

'Nothing! Exactly! And why? Because the greedy two-legs steal it all from right under the bees' noses. And the bees let them! How intelligent is that? Do we want to be like that?'

'No!' came a swell of voices.

'And not content with the honey, there's all the wax,' continued the learned wasp. 'The two-legs take that, too!'

'Yes, but... but...' During the peace and calm of his hours in the olive tree ZX74 had often thought about bees and had never really understood why. Now quite suddenly he realized that the answer had been staring him in the face; perhaps he'd known it all along. 'That's it!'

'What's it?' demanded the principal elder.

It might have been all right if ZX74 had kept it to himself, but having thought the thought, he blurted it out: 'I want to be a bee!'

There was a horrified gasp, louder than any other so far. It was appalling enough that he'd uttered the B-word in the first place, but to wish to be one and to say such was the absolute final straw. One elderly wasp was so shocked that he dropped dead on the spot.

Seeing that he'd made a dreadful mistake, ZX74 fled to his olive tree.

Meanwhile, in the nest there was uproar: 'He's a traitor and should be banished!' cried one wasp.

'He's a disgrace!' cried a second.

'Should have his wings clipped!' cried a third.

'Be stripped of them, more like!' cried a fourth. And so the uproar would have continued had the principal elder not called for silence.

'Clearly,' he said, once quiet had been established, 'we cannot let this go unpunished. I therefore propose that you, Waggle, find this wretched, misguided creature and have a chat with him. Persuade him that if he does not mend his ways—'

'Would that be a nice chat or a nasty chat?' asked Waggle.

'I leave that to you,' said the principal elder. 'All those in favour?' And to signal their solidarity the entire colony buzzed loudly and shook their hind parts as custom demanded.

Word had spread about the olive tree, and in no time at all Waggle and his gang found ZX74 there. Dismissing any thought of a chat — nice or nasty — they took turns to sting him.

'Hold it! The last one's for me!' cried their leader. Proudly he gave his victory waggle, and then with more than a touch of spite in he went for the kill. To their victim this final sting made no difference, for by then he was already well and truly dead.

But now begins the strangest part. A short while after ZX74's departure from this life the olive tree began to flourish as never before. The leaves grew greener, the undersides glowed more silvery, and a year to the day later there appeared – where none had appeared for so long – the first of many olives, rich and purple. Coincidence? Maybe – or then again, maybe not.

The Last Raindrop

How had it come to this? The little cloud had travelled far and wide for so much longer than she cared to remember, and now she was exhausted. More than exhausted, she was in despair. She still hadn't found what she needed to find.

As with all her kind, she had in the past been constantly born and re-born, formed and reformed in a million billion shapes and sizes, forever wafting, billowing or scudding over every part of the lands and seas that stretched in all directions far below. Cold, hot, dry, steamy: what was down there made no difference to her. She went where the wind dictated and did what she was supposed to do, as of course was her duty. Always in the past she had accepted without question her role in the natural order; again as was her duty. But then everything began to change, and she began to wonder.

But how had it come to this? Whether drifting lazily or rushing headlong over whatever lay below, the little cloud had witnessed the changing world: the rising seas; the dry, parched land. How could she not have done? At first what she saw puzzled her, then it dismayed her. Finally, she was outraged. Something was going on down there. She knew she didn't understand it. She knew also that she didn't like it. On the other hand, she told herself not to worry so. Such things had happened many times before; perhaps never so drastically, but they had happened. And always what was not quite right did eventually become right again, and sometimes even better. Or so she thought.

And so she continued to think until that morning on the lakes.

Clouds, as you probably know, have little say in how they grow or where they go. While most don't give two hoots about the whys and wherefores of their cloudhood, there are others who have a preference for the mountains, forests, plains or seas. There are even some who love the polar regions or that harshest of landscapes, the deserts. For this little cloud, if she had a favourite, it was where she was now: above the lakes glistening with freshness and the vast forests of sweet-smelling pine. But the smell that greeted her and other clouds that morning was anything but fresh and sweet.

'Cor, what a stink!' said a neighbouring cloud.

'Get me out of here!' complained another. 'Move on, will you?'

'Don't shove so!' said yet another, irritably. 'I'm going as fast as I can!' But this being where the lakes stretch on and on for miles and miles fast was not fast enough.

As the little cloud stared at the waters below fouled

with rotting organisms she was almost dumbstruck: 'What has happened here?' she gasped.

'Same as what's happening everywhere,' grumbled a bigger cloud. 'Or haven't you noticed?'

'Of course, yes. But it's never been like this,' said the little cloud. 'It will get better again, won't it?'

'Who knows?' said one cloud.

'Who cares?' said another.

'How can you say such a thing?' cried the little cloud.

'Face it, mate. The world's a goner,' said the bigger cloud rather coarsely.

'But this is dreadful!' the little cloud cried. 'We must do something!'

'We? Why would we do anything?'

'Exactly!' said a passing cloud. 'If there's a problem down there—'

'Which there certainly is!'

'—they've brought it upon themselves.'

'Yeah, why bother?' said another cloud. 'As long as we're okay up here.'

'We'll be that all right, if we can get away from this stink!'

'But wait a minute,' said the little cloud, 'isn't it worth saving?'

'This stink?'

'No, the world!'

'Saving it for what? For why?'

The question astonished the little cloud. 'Well, because... because,' she said, 'because it's such a shame, such a waste. All that beauty, all those wonders!'

'What an odd way of thinking,' said the bigger cloud.

'Look, mate. The world's finished. Get used to it, and enjoy yourself,' said the other cloud, and passed on as quickly as he could.

But the little cloud couldn't enjoy herself, and as the weeks went by the stench from the decay that began to cover the land and seas like a thick brown blanket rose higher and higher into the air.

'Is there no hope?' the little cloud cried despairingly. 'Is there no help?'

The other clouds laughed at her distress.

'Why take on so?' said one of them. 'What's it to you what goes on down there?'

'I don't know!' the little cloud admitted. 'But it just seems so... so... awful! Is there really nothing we can do?'

The other clouds laughed more loudly.

From then on, every minute was torture for the little cloud, as the world below suffered and died, till it seemed that whatever life had thrived before would never, could never, thrive there again. Finally, she could stand it no longer. 'No! I won't have it!' she cried. And that's when the idea came to her.

'You're going to do what?' asked a bigger cloud incredulously when the little cloud explained her mission.

'I'm going to save the world,' she insisted.

'Ha! You?' scoffed another cloud which happened to be nearby.

'Well, not just me. All of us.'

'All of us?' the scoffer said, with more than a touch of sarcasm: 'And just how does clever little you propose we do this saving?'

And the little cloud explained as best she could how it had come to her that somewhere down below would be a plant, a fresh green plant which they could save and nurture and–

'You're joking, of course,' the scoffer interrupted.

'No! I feel it. I know it for certain. Don't ask me how, but I do.'

'Well, good luck to you is all I can say. But you're wasting your time!'

'No, wait!' cried the little cloud as the others hurried on their way. 'Won't you help me? Any of you?'

It soon became clear that they were not going to help her. Had it been another time and place, she might have lost heart and given up, but just as the world below had changed, so too had something changed within her: a certainty that all it needed was one green living thing to start again. And she would search for it and find it even if she had to do it all on her own. Just where the answer to the problem had come from is impossible to say; she never knew. But she believed it with a certainty that was rock solid. Well, almost. To every cloud she passed or who passed her, she still continued to ask: 'I'm going to save the world, will you help me?' And always they laughed or scoffed or sneered or excused themselves as being too old, too feeble or too busy. (She could just about understand the first or second reasons, but too busy? Busy with what, she asked herself.)

And so it went on, until one day: 'Sure. I'll help you.'

Her hopes leapt. At last! 'Thank you!' she cried.

'Not so fast,' said the new cloud. 'What's in it for me?'

'What?'

'You can't expect me to waste my precious energy with nothing in return.'

'But it's not for nothing. It's to save the world!'

'Save the–? Why would I do that?'

'It's our duty! Why else are we here if not to water the land, to refresh it and–?'

Then the strangest thing happened. Even as the cloud began to argue that he had far better things to do he started to shrink. 'Hey! What's going on here? What's happening? What have you–?' The next moment, he was gone.

It wasn't only that cloud, but every cloud in sight and beyond, and within a day or two even the biggest and strongest of them had shrivelled to mere wisps. And as they finally disappeared, to the little cloud they had scoffed at they cried, 'Save us! Save us!'

Now the little cloud was really confused. She had watched them disappear to nothingness until the sun-scorched sky was empty. At any moment she expected to go too, but it was not to be. She grew no smaller, and by the end of the day, by the end of the week, of the month even, she was still as she had been before.

At last the wind spoke: 'You wanted to save the world, now's your chance.'

'Why me?' said the little cloud.

'Why not you?' said the wind.

'That's no answer!' the little cloud snapped.

'It's the best you'll get!' snapped the wind in return. 'Now, are you going to do this or not?'

And though she understood even less than before, the little cloud agreed.

'Good,' said the wind. 'I'll do all I can, but in the end it's up to you.'

So the little cloud travelled the world in search of the one green shoot. But as she went her certainty began to fail her. She felt herself weakening, and drop by drop the precious rain within her shrivelled and dried until only one remained.

'Ha!' she imagined the other clouds sneering,

'you think one puny drop of rain is going to make a difference?' No doubt that's what they would have sneered if they'd been there, but they were nowhere now. In that sun-drenched air she was alone, alone with her last raindrop.

She had almost given up hope when far below, piercing the cracked and mottled land, she spied a tinge of colour: so small yet so definitely green. And she knew she had found what she needed.

As she neared her target she explained to her one raindrop the vital task ahead, but she was now so tired she hardly understood what she was saying. Finally, she gasped: 'I've done all I can. It's up to you. Perhaps one day another raindrop will come and then another and another until the land will be reborn and flourish and blossom again as once it did. But go now. Do your duty.'

And she pushed her last raindrop out into the dry suffocating air, and as the raindrop fell and fell the little cloud, too, faded to nothingness.

'I can do this, I can do this!' said the falling raindrop. For a moment she imagined herself the hero of the hour, the day, the future. 'How wonderful that will–'

Just then the wind caught her sharply and she was buffeted to the left. 'Concentrate!' hissed the wind. 'You're not there yet!' Then less sharply the wind blew her to the right, until to her relief she was exactly on course again.

'Thank you!' cried the little raindrop. And straining with all her might to reach the small green shoot, now

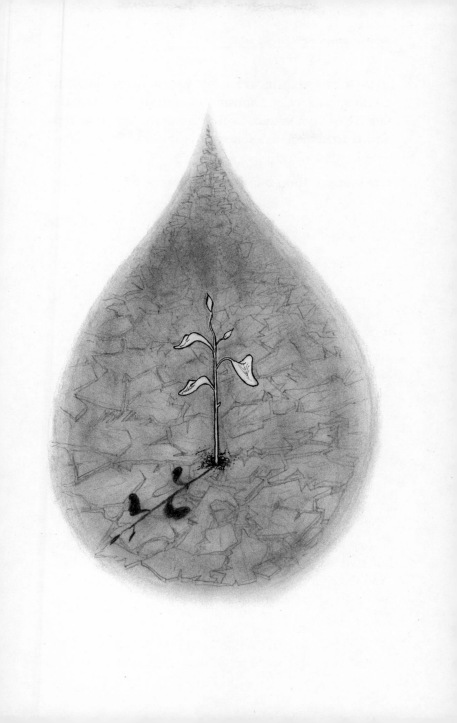

so near and yet still so far, she continued to fall. 'I'm coming,' she cried, almost soundlessly. 'It's not too late... I will get there... I will. It's not too late,' she kept saying to herself. 'It's not too... not too... it's....'

Of course, this is only a story, a simple fiction – and a silly one at that. But what if it were true?

About

About...

**The voice of
learning disability**

Mencap is the UK's leading charity working exclusively with and for people with a learning disability (PWLD), their families and carers. Our vision is a world where PWLD are valued equally, listened to and included. Mencap works tirelessly ensuring that PWLD enjoy the rights and experiences most take for granted, helping them to live their lives with choice, freedom and independence – without judgement and without fear.

A learning disability can happen before, during or shortly after birth and affects the way the brain develops. It is always lifelong. PWLD tend to take longer to learn and may need support developing new skills or understand complex information.

It is important to remember that with the right support most PWLD can lead fulfilling lives. But learning disability is misunderstood by most people. Lack of awareness and understanding leads to prejudice, exclusion and sometimes far worse.

There are 1.5 million PWLD across the UK. When you also consider parents, carers and the wider family network it is estimated that 8 million people are affected by a learning disability. To put this into perspective, every week 350 children are born with a learning disability.

Mencap is dedicated to improving the lives of PWLD. We campaign to change society's negative attitude; influence people who shape policy; and directly empower thousands of PWLD, by delivering a wide range of high quality practical support, from employment services and housing provision to personal support services, leisure opportunities and much-needed advice and information.

For more, go to: www.mencap.org.uk

John Foley

John Foley FRSA is an actor, puzzle setter and audiobook producer. After years of stage work he turned mainly to writing and audio. He has scripted and voiced more than 600 programmes for BBC English/World Service. Other audio work includes adapting numerous plays by writers such as Alan Bennett, Brecht, Ronald Harwood, Ibsen, John Osborne, J B Priestley and Victoria Wood for World Service Drama and Radio 4, and producing for Naxos and Random House unabridged audiobooks of works by Boccaccio, Byron, Wilkie Collins, Dostoevsky, Thomas Hardy, Henry James, Kipling, Salman Rushdie, Anthony Trollope, Sir Walter Scott, Bram Stoker, H. G. Wells, Virginia Woolf and many others. Published work includes several recreational reference books, a volume of musical anecdotes, stories for Disney comics and a number of graded readers for children.

'*Another* Seven Simple and Slightly Silly Stories' is the second of several collections of 'fables', which he began writing some years ago while staying regularly in Hans Andersen's house in Copenhagen.

Grant Cathro

Grant Cathro is an actor, screenwriter and illustration artist. He began his career in his early teens with comedy strip-cartoons for two major Scottish newspapers. The most successful of these, 'The Whirlies' and 'The Kids', ran weekly for many years. A prolific writer for teenage and children's television and with more than 500 produced scripts to his credit, he has been nominated for (and won) BAFTA, Royal Television Society, Writers' Guild of Great Britain and Prix Jeunesse awards. As an artist, Grant illustrated many episodes of BBC's 'Jackanory' and Thames Television's 'We'll Tell You a Story', and for Amber Lane Press has created covers for published plays by Anthony Shaffer, Ronald Harwood, Richard Harris, Bob Larby, Julian Mitchell, Peter Terson, Donald Freed, Maxim Gorky and Chekhov. Over the past decade, he has also provided comedy Christmas cards for the Actors' Benevolent Fund. Grant is currently combining his writing and drawing skills to produce his first illustrated comedy novel.

Still available

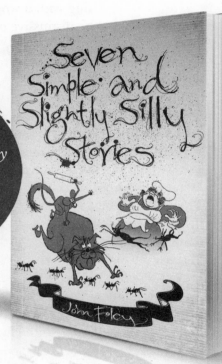

All profits from the sale of *Seven Simple and Slightly Silly Stories* are shared between Macmillan Cancer Support and The Silver Line.

Seven Simple and Slightly Silly Stories

'Delightful and moving with a wonderfully sharp wit, and never again will I be dismissive of the poor old mayfly.'

Jim Broadbent

~

'Funny and thought provoking. Perfect to be read aloud and enjoyed by oldies and young'uns alike. I particularly loved the story of "The Tooth Fairy". A delightful stocking filler.'

Niamh Cusack

~

'Wonderful helpings of whimsy and truth in equal measure. I loved it.'

Julian Fellowes

~

'Every night for the past week I have been reading this extraordinary book and loved every story. Foley has the most glorious imagination and incredibly fertile mind.'

Derek Fowlds

~

'I have just finished reading your 7 simple stories, brilliant. Like all good things I wanted more. I was so moved by the cockroach story. You must MUST do another.'

Derek Griffiths

'These are not only seven simple and slightly silly stories but stupendous, sumptuous and scintillating stories. I hope there's seven or seventy more!'

Mathew Horne

~

'A most absorbing delight from beginning to end. Always witty – but surprisingly sad, too.'

Celia Imrie

~

'With beguiling simplicity, Foley seems to pull off that most difficult of achievements: stories which work at the level of fairytale, which are funny, wry, knowing and yet profound.'

Marion Nancarrow

~

'A delightful book… full of silliness and joy, with a sprinkling of morality to boot. An ideal gift to lift the spirits or to curl up on your own for some self-indulgent mirth!'

Maxine Peake

~

'Neither simple nor silly but wise and witty, John Foley's stories take us back (or is it forward?) into fabulous territory, and Grant Cathro's illustrations light the way. A great read in a venerable tradition!'

Siân Phillips

'Wish I'd had this lovely book in my stocking as a youngster. Brilliant... so great to see the world from a cockroach's point of view. Not many writers have ever attempted that! I now want more please.'

Alison Steadman

~

'Ever spared a thought for the fate of a single sock in a washing machine? Or an ant trying to cross a trunk road in the rush hour? JF's delightful stories sparkle with originality and quirky humour. Perfect escapist reading!'

Juliet Stevenson

~

'I loved these stories. Slightly silly? *Maybe*, but wisdom and compassion lurks within these pages too! I'm looking forward to the next collection.'

Ken Stott

~

'I'm reading John's gently beguiling stories to my children and we think they are fun and thought-provoking. Little gems like "The Mayfly", a joyful call to "seize the day!", seem like an instant classic. I hope more children will enjoy these wonderfully wise tales.'

Dominic West

Coming next!

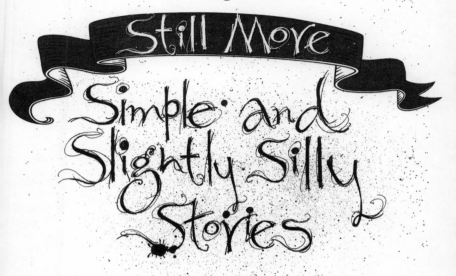

Still More
Simple and Slightly Silly Stories

including **The Nag of Shiraz**, **The Lost Key**,
Spick and Span, **The Bear in the Fifth Floor Flat**,
and **The Shoemaker's Wife**:

Not so long ago and not so very far from here there lived in a village
near the city a shoemaker. As shoemakers go he was probably one of
the worst. He was lazy and incompetent, and the shoes he made were
either too small or too large or, as most often happened, they simply
fell to pieces. And though he knew his shortcomings (for he wasn't
entirely stupid) he made no attempt to improve, and consequently he
barely eked out a living. But somehow, and extraordinary though it
sounds, he managed to snare a wife, and a beautiful and clever one at
that. How that came about, and what happened both to her and to
him is surely a story worth telling. So, if you're ready, here goes…